LIFE PONDERS POETRY

MORE TO PONDER

STEVE E SMITH

**THIRD EDITION

STEVE E SMITH

INTRODUCTION

LIFE
PONDERS
POETRY

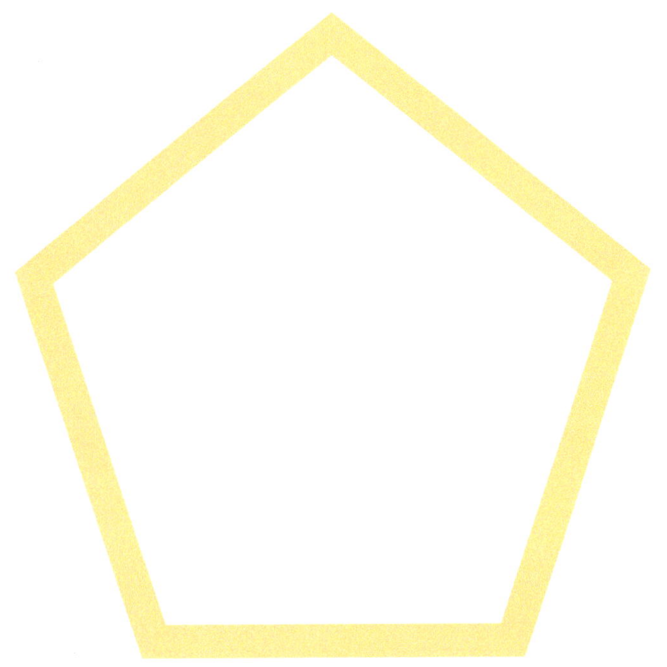

STEVE E SMITH

3

COPYRIGHT

  f

lifeponderspoetry.com
info@lifeponderspoetry.com

INTRODUCTION

ACKNOWLEDGEMENT

The author wishes to express his gratitude towards the publishers for the amazing illustrations presented in this book. The illustrations and artwork have been created and have been adapted with stunning imagery for the poetry.

It is with continued appreciation to all the wonderful people who shared my vision and who continue to follow my work. These awesome folks whom I continue to encounter, love, and cherish, still motivate me to write words that reflect the cycle of life. Thank you all dearly.

Without wonder and insight, acting is just a business.
With it, it becomes creation."

BETTIE DAVIS.

INTRODUCTION

PREFACE

INSPIRATION, LOVE, LUST & DESIRE, REFLECTION, LOSS, AND HUMOUR.

Steve continues to compose his poetry with a passion for implicit expression. Yet, in an artform of verse, rhyme and prose, Steve E Smith continues his quest to give animation to our own human experiences. With true life meaning using his talent created on the following pages, we hope his words may continue to resonate with your life's events.

Steve continues to reflect upon today's human interactions and questions about how they have manifested, to become a new account to follow and adopt. Yet, the passion of his writing still penetrates through with a deliberate methodology to rouse thought to a humanistic rationale for a modern-day philosophy. Words still have potency.

A teacher, musician, and poet, Steve has maintained his devotion to writing and sharing his work with readers from all walks of life. He is dedicated to inspiring the ones who do not feel they have a voice through his words of human experience. Through working in Education and Mental Health, his poetry continues to evolve for the human condition.

With further anticipation from his growing online and global readers, the Steve E Smith community has requested this third book. Thank you to everyone who continues to read his work.

Steve E Smith.
M. Ed.
BA [hons].
Cert. Ed.
Grad. Dip. Music.
Post Grad. SEN.

CONTENTS

COPYRIGHT

ACKNOWLEDGEMENT

PREFACE

INSPIRATION

LOVE, LUST & DESIRE

REFLECTION

LOSS

HUMOUR

MORE TO PONDER

INTRODUCTION

PONDERS
POETRY

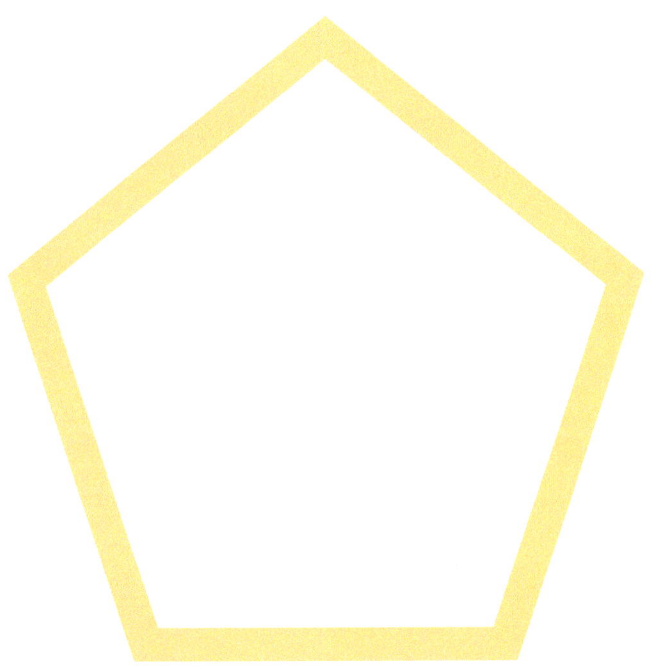

STEVE E SMITH

INSPIRATION

MORE TO PONDER

STEVE E SMITH

THIRD EDITION

"I don't know what my path is yet. I'm just walking on it."

OLIVIA NEWTON JOHN

"If you live in the past that's depression, and if you live in the future that's anxiety. So, you have no choice but to live in the present."

SARAH SILVERMAN

TOMMY.

He's doing his job is our Tommy,
Chasing the drills of war.
Marching proudly along in line,
Cheering crowds galore.

Khaki, brass, with polished boots,
All in unison with military band.
Sequenced step with militarian beat,
Fulfils the crowd so grand.

Off he goes with mighty men,
No fears, no tears to show.
To travel the lands overseas,
Then return? he does not know.

All shaky days are yet to come,
When truth lights that dawn.
To rise again and fight terrain,
To hope he will not mourn.

The ones who stay among the clay,
So still and cold, so wet.
He does not see if this will be,
Unease, to his threat.

Yes, Tommy is doing his bit for the cause,
He stands so proud and straight.
You hope that he will soon see,
His sweetheart, once more, who waits.

Will it be too late?

INSPIRATION

MEMORY.

Take me back to the days of laughter,
With hours under the sky.
Not a device in sight,
The playful summers did fly.

When fears of the foe were less,
When smiles were more abound.
Take me back to those days of glee,
When innocence and joy were found.

The carefree days when we all played,
The soul had much to learn.
Of joyful tunes, we'd hum and croon,
With energies much to burn.

That's not to say, 'a rose-tinted glass,'
Is what we now seek through.
It was just a time when the skies did shine,
We are the chosen few.

MY CHILD.

Just showering my child,
Then preparing for his day.
A countryside walk,
A mundane hour of play.

To see his eyes in awe,
Of the birds and the trees.
Is worth so much more,
When his spirit is free.

For over three decades,
I've taken this walk.
To share conversation,
With limited talk

But I know what he's saying,
I know of his thoughts.
I just look in his eyes,
They say so much more.

This child of mine,
I'm proud of this man.
He's conquered it all,
Just please understand.

That when a child is yours,
And meets a gatekeeper.
I just unlocked all as a key,
With my love so much deeper.

Together we walked through,
Those gates to withhold.
You just haven't a clue,
That he was so bold.

My child, my man,
Is now moving on.
To a brand new future,
With a warmth of the sun.

Well done you.

INSPIRATION

TREASURE OR TRAUMA?

Treasure or Trauma,
Which one is it to be?
You're the one who chooses,
The decisions you make to see.

If you want to live a life,
Without vexation or personal pain.
So, share your love with others,
Then you'll always be the same,
'Treasure'.
Stay away from trauma!

YIN, YANG.

Why does the 'Yina and Yang' hurt so much,
How come it's a transcendental theme?
Where acts of aggression with oppressive pain,
Blights our human dream.

To commit crimes that may lose our human touch,
To de-humanise, 'that one'.
Who gave us grief, who lost belief,
Yet, the 'Yin and the Yang' still won.

An opposite force to seek a score,
To settle the given pain.
To bring out the human love we have,
Through thunder and the rain.

A 'Yin and a 'Yang our choirs have sang,
To balance our nature's wrong.
I hope we will see more mirth with glee,
A Heavenly presence with song.

     INSPIRATION

TO LISTEN.

The world changes,
Day by day.
The questions we ask,
Then, hear them say.

An answer we get,
A story we're told.
To believe in their vision,
Young and old.

But there are the ones,
With a clearer glass.
Who better for the future,
With troubles to pass.

The angels of hope,
The guardians from above,
Who sprinkled this earth,
With humanity and love.

So, don't listen to the narrative,
For doctrinal guide,
Just trust the one,
You feel for inside.

They will take you,
To the right place.
And stand by side,
When troubles to face.

That love you will hold,
That always will pay.
Will always be there,
For ever and a day

INSPIRATION

I will clear your head,
So, when you go home,
Your spirit is fed.
Amen.

STRENGTH.

Strong people are not just borne,
They were made through the storms they faced,
Or even if inherited.

A DNA profile is not always enough to create such a being.
It's the man or woman standing there,
You are all just plainly seeing.

They have gained that chaliced cup,
They hope to gain your regard.
They hope to see you back on top,
They'll always help you start.
Keep going!

KINDRED SOLE.

Kindred spirit just stopped by,
To smile and say, "Hello".
She told me of her secret thoughts,
Mixed up with glee and woe.

A spiritual sole was clear to see,
Through the windows of her eyes.
A woman strong, a warrior she,
With sunshine there to rise.

Each morn would come to share her steps,
With friends of canine kin.
To chase in fields of grasses wept,
A stoic woman within.

FADED LIGHT.

A light begins to dim,
One day it might just switch off.
A memory, a face, for who you are,
May never be enough.
But you carry as a beacon of light,
Be their angel from morn till night.

ABSENCE OF HOPE.

It's the absence of hope that absorbs us.
It's the absence of love that takes its toll.
When ways to a world does not applaud us,
To preserve ways of love for these souls.

A fear of less hope will emerge its ugly head,
A dark cloud will hover from the sky.
A door then appears for you to open,
Stay clear, and I will tell you why.

Come back into the light and keep on hoping,
Tis the only precious gift that we possess.
To resist and to fight without moping,
You will the pass this life's lesson test.
Amen.

THE ONE.

You will meet that one someday,
That dream person who loves you dear.
Together you will work rest and play,
You will share your spirits without fear.

The journey seems tiresome, dragging along,
You still trundle through every hour.
Then, with surprise with Heavenly eyes,
You bloom as imposing as nature's flower.

From seeds sewn some moons ago,
With alignment of stars, you will meet.
And pow! somehow, with love to bestow,
Your meet and greet is complete.

FUTURE

Your future seems clouded,
By the ones in position.
They appear to assure you,
With every decision.

With policy and philosophy,
That surely comes your way.
But you just can't stop, and you wish to flop,
Again, a darker day.

Yet, I promise you just take control,
You are the helm of your destiny.
Whatever happens, whatever becomes,
You are still the one who's free.

Maintain your belief and follow that star,
Because you are loved and will go far.
Retain your craft and don't be daft,
I promise you, you're not the last.
To get there.
Believe in yourself.

ICE

A polar bear came floating by,
On a little isle of ice.
He waited and just kept still,
That helped to pay the price.

For that longer journey on his raft,
Of snow and ice to thaw.
He waited so he could reach land,
Yet sadly, there was no more.

Of lands to roam to call his home,
Where he could just roam free.
The lands were bare, it wasn't fare,
There was nothing left, you see.

He just kept going with cheeks glowing,
The bear he never gave in.
The waters kept flowing and he kept showing,
His soul was stronger within.

For miles, he sailed towards a land,
That came nearer and closer each day.
The waters still cold and he remained bold,
A feeling this place was to stay.

He jumped onto land of snow without sand,
He knew he had reached the end.
His self-belief compromised grief,
His vision would not bend.

He got there!

SHELTER

Welcome to my new home, it's built for one,
It shelters from the rain.
My bed is soft under a nylon roof,
Each day is never the same.

My mobile home rests a new day dawn,
To set up camp each day.
A brand-new door I have each night,
No rent I need to pay.

Under moon and stars, I'm placed so far,
Away from my last street.
I mingle in with new folks' dim,
New friends I long to greet.

This home of mine seeks a daily town,
But I just get moved on again.
No fixed abode and still on the road,
With rise and fall of sun.

Yet, I know that promised land,
Will soon become that sight.
Where I can rest live and play,
A home for day and night.

So, I tell you all if you ever fall,
Just get back up and march.
Just keep going each day when snowing,
You will find a brand-new start.

Tomorrow will be a better day.

RANT

Do you internalise that one who hurls a rant?
Do you pity those words of war?
Do you wish they could be much more fun?
Do your eyes drop down to the floor?

Be wise and warm and weather the storm,
Be the one who asserts wisdom.
For gentle words with no hearts torn,
May build a better kingdom.

Evade the grief with one belief,
They are the ones who menace.
Avoid their presence who maintain bad essence,
For them, they just like to play tennis.
It's a game to them.

RELATION

That relation is always there,
The one who insists on creating a stir.
Who chooses to offend any reasonable logic,
With results that became quite a bit tragic.

The,pain and hurt they like to give,
Lingers long to those who live.
But just move on and smile with the sun,
Be happy you are with, the one you love.
Keep smiling!

DAILY

A daily prayer,
A daily thought,
Will bring a happy day.
A daily hug,
A daily kiss,
Will help you rest and play.

GREATEST GIFT

The greatest gift to give a child,
Is to bestow them self-esteem.
The greatest love to present a child,
Is to help them with their dreams.

To show them there is always away,
To achieve that personal goal.
To help them see they are unique,
In mind, body and soul.

The greatest gifts to grant a child,
Is show them all to see.
They are all special living souls,
I'm sure you'll all agree.

STRANGE EXISTANCE

The earth is not round,
The world is just square.
The sky is not up,
The Heavens are down there.

The clouds are not white,
They're green, pink and red.
The sea is not blue,
It's yellow instead.

The cars drive backwards,
To where they have been.
The plane it does fly,
To a wonderful dream.
The people all flown,
Have all seen the light.
They all just can't wait,
Until their next flight.

So, things we can't change,
New facts we must learn.
Thank Heavens there's existence,
For love, so to yearn.
Love Conquers All.

IMAGINE

Just imagine it's pink,
Just imagine it's blue.
Just imagine any colour you want,
And make your dreams come true.

Just imagine it's short,
Just imagine its' long.
Just imagine you're the best in the world,
And always having a ball.

Just imagine you're happy,
Just imagine you're sad.
Just imagine being good all the time,
And never being bad.

Just imagine.

TODAY

Today is just another day,
And there will be tomorrow.
Today is the day you succeed,
And do away with sorrow.

Don't look back to blame and curse,
Those days are truly gone.
So, do reflect and do detect,
The days that glowed and shone.

A day, an hour before nightfall,
Is all you ever need.
To find your dream and win supreme,
This is the day you are so freed.
From yesterday.

            INSPIRATION

FIGURINE

A figurine stands proudly in your garden,
Facing whatever is to come.
Rain, hail, wind or snow,
Its daily battles are won.

That little fairy maintains a smile,
With wings spanned and still.
Colours glisten and shine each day,
To sustain its strength and will.

A lesson for us all to take,
Each day, you must embrace.
To face it all, whatever might fall,
And present your being with grace.

LITTLE BIRD

A little bird came down one day,
He smiled with a crooked beak to say.
"Have you heard the news today,
That now you star in a bright new play".

Soon you will be that chosen one,
And folk will want to share.
The joys you bring into our life,
For those who really care.

Your mission was to be with us,
We have all waited for you.
And know that you will lead the way,
In everything we do.

EVERMORE

The love will find,
Will be with you ever more.
Whatever you do.

Do not show them a door,
A door to gloom with a troubled road.
Be the one to share the load,
With all life's gifts and love bestowed,

Stay together, both in tune,
Show the one stars, sun and moon.
Dance in the garden,
Sing in the woods.
Give your all,
Your worldly goods.

The gift of love,
It can never be lost.
Treasure, forever,
At any cost.

Then you will find happiness.

FORGIVENESS

The man behind the stick,
The woman who just sits by.
The child in the middle,
Just begins to cry.

Back then it made no concept of sense,
Those voices of descent.
The trembles from your knee,
Was there for all to see.

An early childhood day,
When you purely had no say.
The wrongs and rights of childhood,
Interruption from fun and play.

What on earth was wrong?
With man and woman of care.
When all they had to offer,
Contusion with added despair.

Yet, they bestowed you right from wrong,
They show you the side not to be.
And later, it began to make sense,
A space was there for you to agree.

Your future aspirations beheld,
To how you will live your life.
And become a brand-new template,
Without the hurt, gloom with strife.

Be thankful you are strong,
Don't manifest to blame your past.
You have become a special being,
The one, who's love will last.

You became that one to show love.

GREENER

When you see the grass is green and lush,
Which beckons you towards a fervent sight.
Do take care not to be in a rush,
So, you're the one who'll bite.

Is your vision askew with hope?
Is it clouded there to blank your scope?
Your perception and desire may feel not right.
Please be beware before your flight.

Keep on flying you'll get there,
To lay in a promised land.
With a tear and a smile and in a short while,
You'll begin to understand.

The grass does not need to be green,
This world is a bigger place.
For a mountain, desert, forest scene,
With awesome vista to face.

The world is not just green.

NEW DAY

My day of Spring today,
My page turned overleaf for a better read.
My boat came in to deliver goods,
My flowers bloomed from hopeful seed.

My dreams have come true,
I now can start anew.
To raise my game,
To be with you.

WRONGED

Try not to blame the one who wronged you,
It's a lesson to make you strong.
Don't cry with woes bestowed you,
You can still sing your song.

GUIDE

In your career, please lend me your ear,
For the ones you will guide may bite.
Take care that you're free, and hope you will see,
It may be a turbulent flight.

Those ice-cold snarls may come your way,
Be sure to know it isn't you.
It's another test against the rest,
They choose to see you blue.

No matter how long you walked the path,
To experience a lesson in morning class.
You will still be pelted with wrath and pain,
Some folks are still the same.

So, keep on going and maintain sight,
Be the person you really are,
With so much joy you give to folk,
You're still a shining star.

PATRICIA

Patricia the swan swam by one day,
She looked so graceful and calm.
With elegant glide and cannot be denied,
That she was graced with charm.

Her feathers preened so pure and white,
Her neck was long and slim.
No splash from her to wet her hair,
Patricia could certainly swim.

No sailing ship or cruising trip,
Could sail the way she could do.
As Patricia is being the only one,
Who glides serenely, so true.

DRIFT

The days seem to drift apart,
Flying by as rolling reels.
Flickering images to yesterday's events,
Precious time to come and to heal.
It will get better.

HAVE YOU EVER?

Have you ever had that feeling,
That you want to run away?
When the cards that you were dealt with,
Didn't have much to say.

The forecast looks so bleak,
The numbers don't add up.
That vision you were dreaming,
Would really cheer you up.

So, take a trip to Paris,
Throw the cards away in the bin.
Pour your-self a glass of wine,
And maybe have a gin.

With Ooh La La's and music sweet,
You'll soon be dancing on your feet.
Buy your-self a new pack of cards,
Then have your-self a brand-new start.

Tour the city and shed the pity,
From your bright new self.
So, be the one to share your fun,
And you will find new wealth.
Keep Going!

INSPIRATION

FIXED

I tell you now with an open heart,
That you, yes you, can be fixed.
Just hang on there with resolute stare,
No longer emotions mixed.

With words of woe thrown your way,
With arrows of sharpened aim.
Keep that love and maintain a stance,
It will never be the same.

IMPASSE

If it doesn't work,
Just let go,
The impasse may hold your march.
Stomp ahead with open mind,
Retune, reframe, re-start.

JOURNEY

Your journey may take longer,
More miles upon the clock.
With bumps and potholes on the way,
But you will never stop.

Rain and wind interrupt your voyage,
But rainbows will emerge.
With skies that smile along the miles.
You'll always feel an urge.

To continue your journey.

DREAMS

"The world is your oyster",
They used to say.
Go live your dreams,
Just work, laugh and play.

Don't fall for all,
That doom and gloom.
Your dreams will happen,
But not so soon.

You will learn patience,
You will learn to wait.
That Holy Grail you're seeking,
May just come with fate.

Yet, it doesn't come easy,
You still must toil.
To figure out how to gain,
To how to re-coil.

And start over again,
Without, the 'mistake',
Then you will enjoy,
The ones without fake.

The Holy Grail,
A fantasy to some.
But you will be booming,
With much more to come.

MY CHILD'S JOURNEY

Dear chid, continue the journey,
make your tomorrow today.
Enjoy the freedom for you endowed,
gate crash this world with your stay.

Your visit here, for all of you,
will for ever succeed.
Show resilience to any cloud,
sew in new fresh planted seed.

Your roads ahead, your mountainous climb,
will be yours to overtake.
Do not be deterred by words inferred,
we all can make mistakes.

Seize your venture, be that mentor,
let all know to grasp your word.
See you make good, and understood,
and that you'll not be scared.

Grab the moment, empower your spirit,
soar to wonderous skies.
Do the grind with all mankind,
then soon, you will, just fly.

INSPIRATION

LOVE, LUST & DESIRE

"The future belongs to those who believe in the beauty of their dreams."

ELEANOR ROOSEVELT.

IN MY CLASP

To share your lips,
With urgent need.
To fix my gaze on you.
To enter your garden of raptured bloom,
To taste your wine is so true.

To share my perspiration of joy,
To share my breathless gasp.
To feel your warm embrace again,
I have you in my clasp.
And will, never let you go.

SORCERESS

To gaze, to hold, to breathe so bold,
To brush aside those days when cold.
The warmth with you is flaming today,
I'm here for you, and I will forever stay.

To whisper words of sheer delight,
To let you be my queen of night.
A darling sorceress that you are,
To share your dreams that took us far.

Yet, within another time frame,
You're lost in space.
The pain I can't have you,
I remain in a place.
Of indeterminate state.

MAGICAL.

The words I wonder are just for you,
These lines are placed in verse.
Are for you - my darling one,
Not seeing you is my curse.

I long to share my delights with you,
I crave to have you near.
My magic wand is here to show,
My sorcery with no fear.

A spell, no potion could ever stop,
The desires I'd share with you.
To entwine your thighs against my skin,
Tis sure you need no clue.

My blood runs hot against your kiss,
My aching wand is proud.
To show you a spell and I will tell,
To hear you gasp aloud.

So, my sweet please can I treat,
You to a magic hour.
And seduce your being my love un-freeing,
To lain with you these hours.

CELTIC WOMAN.

My little Celtic woman,
Queen of the tribe.
To lay into your being,
To quench, to imbibe.

The juices from your cup,
From you, a scented woman of desire.
To engage with my thrust,
To share a passion with fire.

The hot steamy lips - that kiss,
Your beautiful reddened lips.
The tongue to explore,
The you I yearn for more.

I will wait till the end of time,
When you would welcome me in.
I would stand at your door,
Until your heart I can win.

NAKED.

The naked flesh is all beyond any attire to wear,
No need to dress, as all I do is stare.

To absorb the beauty of your physical hold,
I bow to thee forever,
My love is sold.

On you.

OMNISCIENCE.

Omniscience an aura only you can give,
A presence of love is such a precious gift.
Your darlingness of woman only I can see,
My life is so complete when I'm with thee.

You are forever there in my day,
I so wish you were here to stay.
To feel your tenderness of delicate hand,
Easing my pain only you understand.

Your manifestation is never far away,
I see you darling night and day.
Your spirit is embedded in my soul,
When with you I can't control.

So, just to tell you, "You're there in my mind",
I see the beauty; I could never be blind.
To your divine radiance, you're here with me,
You are all that I want, you are all that I see.

PICTURE OF YOU.

If I had a picture of you,
It would be on my wall to show.
For the world to see that you and me,
Are forever together and know.

That no matter where you darling be,
No matter where you show.
The Heavens sing my love to you,
Tis there wherever you go.

The miles across the land and sea,
The hours are far apart.
Yet, I can never let you go,
You're forever - within my heart.

So, darling this is my message to you,
My words do say it all.
The sweetest, dearest angel you are,
The you, the one I call -
"My sweetest love".

SEVEN STAGES.

For the eternal woman,
For stages of her life.
They are not just there - to summon,
As someone, as a wife.

Though a maiden she may be,
A sweetness of a being.
You are wanting of a wife,
Is that just all you are seeing?

A mother for your children,
The solace of your home.
If you would sin to hurt her,
Then you will be alone.

The mystique would surely flourish,
Her guile would bring you pain.
Along with darkened clouds,
With thunder and the rain.

Her age of crone would be a cloak,
Her sorcery could be used.
But only if you ever,
Chose to serve abuse.

A woman of wisdom is she,
A woman of insight with sage.
Tis fortunate that she chose you,
To share her morning's page.

To read her as truly yours,
A guardian angel so true.
And then a warrior princess,
Whatever? She'll care for you.

Then to share in a dream,
To embrace her and to feel,
Whenever you are down,
She'll be there to heal.

Today and tomorrow.

BEGUILE.

A woman of beguile and beauty,
Came to me one day.
To share her joys of existence,
To share her passion for play.

To witness this Heavenly vision,
To hear those words of joy.
To embrace her charms with open arms,
A savoured warmth employ.

Thank you for that wonderful hour,
When your eyes beguiled me so.
Thank you for your sweetest words,
Our love will grow to show.
Thank you.

LAY AWAKE.

So, I lay awake to think of you,
You're in my mind since half past two.
To imagine your touch to feel so much,
To share your love, so warm and true.

AN ODE FOR YOU

To eat, to imbibe and share with you,
A precious hour, so overdue.
To now enjoy minutes to listen,
with timbres soft with eyes that glisten.

To tell a tale of how you perceive,
To internalise and solemnly believe.
That in yourself and in your faith,
Which validates no need to wait.

You're true and kind I'm certainly not blind,
I see the 'you' - I hear the mind.
Your heart is good, your resolve so strong,
Your guarded self it won't be long.

Til you tell me all and share your soul,
With spiritual ease, you will not fall.
You rise above the pleasing eye,
You've learnt to sustain and get by.

Your path to follow, you've learned so well,
Your compass true, I can tell.
So, the future road may hold for you,
A bumpy track, a stone in shoe.

Darling, I tell you, "You are a divine being".
You absorb a faith; with all you are seeing.
I hope that now you attain my stance,
A regard for you with pleasing glance.
Goodnight darling, and you sleep tight,
A new day comes with morning light.

BREAKFAST THOUGHT

Having breakfast, having toast,
A cup of tea with you, my host.
I'm with you now with your embrace,
But soon I hope to share your space.

NEW DAY.

A new day for you,
A new day for me.
But still I wonder,
If you'll ever be free

To share the passion,
To share an embrace.
It would be Heavenly,
Just to see your face.

But across the miles,
And across the days.
We do still retain -
Our True Love Ways.

LONG NIGHT.

I have set sail for another long night,
You, my precious are still in my sight.
Even when I retreat to my empty bed,
Thoughts of you, darling are still in my head.

A BIRTHDAY WISH.

A birthday wish, tis only for you,
And hope and pray, your dreams come true.

Another year comes and then it goes,
You embrace the highs to dispel the lows.

Your beauty still shines to radiate a room,
I will be there, to see you soon.

Happy Birthday!

MISSION.

The moon with stars may gravitate to you,
To expose your goodness therein.
The wind and rain will give you no pain,
The sun shines warmth on your skin.

The clouds go by and never do cry,
When hovering above your vision.
But the magnetic force begins this course,
Divinity of passion my mission.

ENCOUNTER.

We encounter those who touch our soul,
Who sprinkle all their love.
But you're the one who makes me whole,
An angel from above.

MOVED BY YOU.

I was moved by you,
The first time you sat and gave me an eye.
My heart pounded, my tummy tingled,
My aching brow perspired.

You sent me to another world,
A place where Heaven and joy.
Gave me a reason to be with you,
No words could ever destroy.

This devotional love I possess for you,
You're the one who was gifted to me.
Please my darling I'll never let go,
You're the purest woman I see.
I was moved by you.

BEDTIME.

Soon I'll be in my comfy bed.
To lay down and rest my weary head.
Then close my eyes and dream of you,
To have you close till morning new.

LOVELY DAY.

Have a lovely day my sweet,
Without your kiss, I'm not complete.
The hours go by each empty day,
When I think of passions and how to play.
With you.

THE BOX

This box of treasures,
A gift to you.
It will tell you stories,
From my heart so true.

Each item represents,
A part, a history of me.
These cherished memories of my past,
Are yours to keep and see.

Treasures, traumas,
From my past.
To share my love,
To ever last.

So, treat with care,
And please embrace.
These gifts from me,
Together we'll face,
Tomorrow.

WITHOUT LOVE.

Someone who is not in love,
Could not be a beacon of light to others.
How can their soul be charged.
How can a flag dance without a whispering breeze.
How can the sun, shine without heat.
How do the stars sparkle without twinkle.
How do the seas, wave without a tide.
Love is all we have and to cherish,
as a life of its own.
Without love, we do not exist –
as whole.

MADE TO LOVE

You are made to love,
You are made to bare.
To show to others,
The art of care.

You are a human form,
For all to see.
That we are created,
To be you and me.

Without the hurt,
Without the grief.
Just be aware,
To share a belief,
That you were made to love.

CHRISTMAS MESSAGE.

A Christmas message just for you,
To show how much I care
The hours and days away from you,
I really cannot bear.

So, I send this Blessing on to you,
And hope that you keep true,
I'm still here with wine and beer,
You just haven't got a clue.
"How much I care".

OPENING.

Give me an opening for me to complete,
Let me explore that space to fill.
With words and actions to secure my lust,
For me to entice with equated thrill.

The thrill and wanting of your need,
The drive to share within.
With urgent cure to give you more,
My heart is yours to win.

BLACKBERRY FEAST.

A blackberry rush is sweet with desire,
Full of vitamin C with untold passion.
A blackberry kiss will stoke the fire,
I hope it suits today's new fashion.

To share a blackberry feast with your chosen one,
So specially carefully selected.
To dine and eat to share completely,
Feeling spiritually connected.

No other fruit could be as this,
No other taste can be your kiss.
You are the one I choose for mine,
You are my blackberry feast –
my food, my wine.

ALL FOR YOU

It's all for you,
Every word, every phrase.
To me, you amaze with spellbound gaze.
It's all for you, my darling sweet woman.
I just never saw it coming,
Your spirit did summon.
My submission to you I give.
With you, I want to live.
It's all for you.

RATHER

I would rather see you laugh than cry,
I would rather say 'hello' than goodbye.
I would rather see the sky so blue,
I would rather share my nights with you.

I would rather share your kiss each day,
I would rather have you here to stay.
I would rather be Laine in your arms,
I would rather succumb to your charms.

So, please do look around to see,
I am here for you, I plea.
It's taking so long so I've written my song,
I'd love rather if you would come to me.
I'm still singing!

THANK YOU

Thank you for choosing me,
Thank you for your care.
Thank you for your company,
Thank you for being there.

Thank you for sharing my days,
Thank you for your love.
Thank you for your darling ways,
You're sent from Heaven above.

PASSIONS

The hands may struggle,
Through kiss and cuddle,
They wander to a zone.
When passions on full alert,
Then both as one, atoned.

The breath does pant,
With dress so scant,
Beguiled beneath your charm.
Perfumed flesh sets me alight,
Never a cause for alarm.

I will just settle back,
To be back on track,
Yet my heart still races on.
Oh my gosh, I need you so,
Even when you've gone.

DELICIOUS TONES

Delicious tones from your frame,
Glowing moonbeams with prismed flame.
The window is our beam of light,
Our stage scene set for dramas of night.

Fire embers quietly with stuttered spark,
Adds hues with shades to your skin.
The perfect act, scene one, action,
Then, I am gently within,
You.

REFLECTION

"Don't judge each day by the harvest you reap,
but by the seeds that you plant."

ROBERT LOUIS STEVENSON

NO GUARENTEE.

Flicking through pages of moons gone by,
Decades of love, then to laugh and to cry.
We have all visited a place to be,
With family and friends without guarantee.

The chances we take, the choices we make.
But I tell you now,
"It was never a mistake",
With you!

CHILDREN.

The soul is healed, being with children,
They innocently show the way.
Their regard unconditioned with warmth and care,
Will shine for you through play.

Eureka will come to spark the light,
To be your guiding star.
A new way forward will show the one,
They'll help that 'you' go far.

SAINT.

You can see a Saint anywhere,
That gravitation of human beings.
You can see the shaman who really cares,
Who shows you light to heal with meaning.

Who provides that Heavenly human touch,
In an indecent world that's ready to crush.
You can see a Saint anywhere,
The one who heals, the one who shares.
His love.
With you.

YOUTH.

Is 'youth' today a negative word?
Why are the young deemed so bad?
Think very hard before you judge,
I tell you, "Don't be sad".

There are still the ones who do their best,
Who tries to work so hard?
But are they being placed to perhaps fail?
When given that in -apropos start.

Even if they passed exams,
And succeeded to degree.
A lifetime paying, back the fees,
Whenever will they be free?

A Diploma gained, then degree,
Is all that was achieved.
Was this the best transaction?
It's very hard to believe.

We need more hands-on work,
The ratchet, spanner, and bolt.
No exams that cause a jam,
To lead to this revolt.

Will our youth have the chance,
To think as one who'll be?
With self-esteem to live the dream,
Whenever will they be free?

OLD SOUL.

I think I have been here before,
As every time I open the door,
I feel as though you're standing there,
I sense your spirit, none can compare.

This old soul gave me inspiration,
With spiritual guise for installation.
These feelings stop me from going there,
Commitments now, are creating despair.

The phobia of rejection,
Failure and doubt,
Resonate in my head,
They just seem to shout.

So, now hiding under the warm duvet,
Trying to sleep my problems away.

Will I go up or will I go down?
This old sage can give me my crown,
Because now can I see,
I've been a clown.

ALLOTMENT.

My allotment is a wonderful haven for happiness.
Where I grow more,
But my troubles grow less.

A therapeutic dream,
A counsellor of green.
Where birds sit along,
With a chorus of glean.

When I walk home,
After my day.
My heart's no longer heavy,
My Heavenly stay.
Where green fingers play.
My close of the day.
Perfect.

SOMEONE'S CLOUD.

Be a rainbow in someone's cloud,
Stand beside them and shout aloud.
That you are there, their trusted friend,
And you'll be with them right to the end.

Show them the way to that golden mile,
Bring them joy and make them smile.
Be a friend forevermore,
Let them know that your door.
It is always open!

REFLECTION

BABY SITTING MUM.

I'm so weary, not sleeping at night,
Looking after Mum keeps me in sight.
One eye open, the other eye closed,
She has a little wonder on her tip toes.
I get her back to bed and tuck her feeble frame in,
Then, only an hour later, I did it all over again.
Night, night, mum.

QUITE SIMPLE

It is quite simple, really,
All we need to do is share.
Are we shown from infant days?
Are we shown how to care?

To divide our thoughts to others around us,
To smile and take their hands.
And show them a way through rest and play,
I'm sure they will understand.

Yet, as we grow and as we learn,
We see a different earth.
Is greed or wealth now prioritised,
To show how we deem its worth?

Worth to them is power and gem,
They are never satisfied.
It's only when they cause mayhem,
That hearts and souls do cry.

So, can we learn to share,
And learn to love and pray,
I hope it's all worthwhile,
Forever and a day.
It's quite simple really.

CONCERN

Many trees make a copse,
Many trees make wood.
Many trees make a forest,
When removed, they make a flood.

Many flowers make a bunch,
Many flowers make a lee.
Many flowers make a garden,
For all mankind to see.

Take away their freedom,
And everyone will learn.
It is our regard for duty,
We must all show concern.

SNOW

So, snow has come to spread its white.
Came passing through in the dead of night.
A carpet bright with glow in the air,
So, I drive and hope I get there.

WHY?

Dear God, why don't you listen,
To wisdom from others?
Who share their mantra,
As a community mother.

They don't preach or scorn,
To serve a point.
They are so Blessed,
With foresight to anoint.

We reap what we sew,
We gain what we learn.
The blame game appears,
In cycle to return.

IVY

The ivy navigates its twisted twine,
To bind the knobbly bark.
Twisting with a pleasure of play,
From dawn to dusk then dark.

It does not need to plan or plot,
The genetic code will guide.
Throughout the years without a fear,
Its mission could never hide.
Its quest.

THEY

They certainly have a claim on you,
They proclaim their path is the only way.
They fight and curse and conquer you,
I hope they seek council to pray.

They shout, 'This is the only way!'
They have no faith in you.
How do we conclude what is true?
To what is deemed as freedom.

Bloodshed, loss and death all suffered for you,
They are never satisfied.
To deny others of their freedom,
For there is no shelter to hide.

They claim their victory is supreme,
Yet, slain with violent words.
Even each other with child and mother,
Who pray for you when scared.

They choose a war with a roll of a dice,
They want you there in Khaki stance.
To shoot a stranger without a price,
They use our souls to take their chance.

EXAM

This is now in exam conditions,
It is not a sociable event.
So do this test with ardent zest,
And reap from the hours you spent.

On revised text with questions,
Of all the subjects learned.
So, do well, then ring that bell,
The corner you have turned.

CIRCUS. [NO REASON].

The innocence of a child taken away.
Like taking candy from a baby.
A light, snuffed out, and not knowing why?

No reason was given, no motive in hand,
Just a circus of conquest to visit our land.
With their microphone, camera and flash bulb too,
I so hope they remember when they are through.

They'll leave behind a broken street,
Dwelled by folk no longer complete.
With broken hearts, with fragile smile,
They were there to weep in single file.

Now shadows of beings,
Ghosts of their past event.
Etched in hearts and minds,
Without relent.

Behind a trail of broken hearts,
Behind, memories to never forget.
Behind, tears to shed each day,
Behind, a devotion of sweet regret.

We will pray for you each night,
When that circus leaves your street.
Their lenses now all shuttered,
But please don't take defeat.

We are all with you each night and day,
We'll all come around to skip and play.
We'll dance as a child with laughter too,
We'll still be there when the circus is through.

For Southport.

MOTHER NATURE.

I heard Mother Earth talk one day,
While ambling down the path.
I heard her cry and sob for me,
She poured out her grief and wrath.

I heard her talk while I walked,
She told me of her sorrow.
Each time I paced along this earth,
Her compass was to follow.

The Mother Earth growled this day,
To let her passions pour.
Earthquakes, lightning, volcanoes, and rain,
She could take no more.

"For Heaven's sake, why do men make,
A pact to loot this globe?
They take its jewels and then move,
To leave Mother Nature cold".

I listened with care and with glare,
To all that was around.
I heard her weep right through my sleep,
At night with eerie sound.

Soon the morn with new day borne,
I gave my solemn word.
That no more man shall do no harm,
With tearful eyes so blurred.

Questions came: who was to blame?
For all the scars left behind.
"It's simple really and is clearly,
They take and are so blind",

To consequence, there's weak defence,
No one can account for greed.
Their signed papers with corporate capers,
To exclude Mother Nature's needs.

                    REFLECTION

WHAT HAPPENED?

We show them how to use a spoon,
We show them how to eat.
We show them how to potty train,
We show them love complete.

The way to mix and socialise,
The way to greet and play.
The way to talk, laugh and cry,
The way to kneel and pray.

We wanted them to get along,
We wanted their gaze with a smile.
We wanted to share their happiness,
We wanted to share a mile.

When no longer a teen,
They choose to stay at home.
They are waited on hand and foot,
And yet they moan.

Whatever happened to twenty-one,
Whatever did go wrong?
Why did they choose to stress?
Why do they stay so long?

Mmmmm?

ANGEL

An angel came down from Heaven one day,
Just to say "Hello",
He looked so fine with radiant shine,
With open wings and a hallowed glow.

He asked if I could help,
As in Heaven, they are short-staffed,
I stood dumbfounded without a sound,
I thought, "he's just having a laugh".

This angel said, "We need more folk",
To make us laugh, to make a joke,
There's now a trait for history,
When doom and gloom create misery.

We need more Angels in our team,
To smile with glee for all.
We are there day and night,
And we'll be ready for when you call.

I'm just not ready yet.

NO CLUE

I beg of you to lend an ear,
Yet, all you do is dish out fear.
You smile and say, "it will be alright",
Yet, I cannot sleep at night.

Where is your compass?
Tell me where is it pointing to?
Please, just walk a day in my shoes,
You have not got a clue!

ABANDON

To abandon that dearest being,
Without conscience is not the way.
That long standing tower of might.
Who helped pull you from a dark place.
To reflect to act in present tense with scorn.
This conflict with the beneficence you owned.
Tis not a manner for a way forward,
For any mortal.
Then perform with transference.
Please take back the askew of text.
Accept your own fragility with erroneous view.
Wake up to see your own flaw before others.
Then, you will move forward,
With a brighter heart.
Your light will never fade for others,
The real you, you will discover.

TO SHOP

Is there a limitation of voice,
To purchase without any choice.
You get what is there on a shelf,
For a cost only placed, for their wealth.

It's an increasing weekly shop,
And so, tiring I just want to flop.
No enjoyment at the till,
With money to spend and still

It's just not enough.

SOLLITUDE

The solitude of a wooden companion,
Resting there, inert, still and cold.
Never again to be graced by your warmth,
Inanimate, cushioned frame from days of old.

Was once a centre piece for laughter and mirth,
Was once there for lively debate.
Was once the seat of parliament,
Was once there for you to state.

Opinioned narrative to the core,
This room would echo more and more.
Your voice to share our fireside kiss,
The room is empty, and I still miss,
You.

As I stare at this chair of wisdom,
I talk to ghosts of yesterday.
When cups of teas and pieces of cake,
For hours we would stay.

Your spirit is still there.
When I come to this empty room,
Perfumed memories fill the air,
Together we would croon.

An empty room an empty chair,
Will forever be your shrine.
Thank you darling for choosing me,
Thank God, that you were mine.

REFLECTION

GHOSTED LOVE.

A ghost of love emerged one day,
From a long time past when we would play.
A scene from Shakespeare of true romance,
We laid together in riveted trance.

The years came back and told me how,
Of that Angelic being to prompt me now.
That the heart still beats in double time,
When you are near radiance shine.

To light the way into your arms,
To seduce my actions with feminine charms.
You say, you chose the one you love,
But you are here to say your love,
Is for me, still.

WHAT HAPPENED

What has happened to a sense of purpose?
Do we all have a map to a wonderland of joy?
What happened to our journey of dreams,
Now diminished for our girls and boys.

That golden dream with awe and plan,
And now been replaced by school exams.
It seems, that every boy and girl,
Will have to wait to see the world.

DEAR GOD

Dear God, I ask you why.
There are children who fret and cry.
Why don't you just lend a hand?
And comfort them to understand.

Those little souls who shed a tear,
Are existing now through hunger and fear.
They travel the lands on foot with pain,
To try and find their dreams again.

Their homes are gone, and their neighbours too,
All they need is a word from you.
To assure them that, they will get through,
Why are they, so sad and blue?

So, Dearest Lord and maker of man,
My entreaty to you.
To relieve their pain, so they again,
May walk-in brand-new shoes.

YESTERDAY'S TUNE

The guitar still plays tunes of yesterday,
The notes and chords still chime.
With yesterday's croon and melodious tune,
Way back to a glorious time.

When music was an art form deemed,
It was the soul of man.
Yet, today, notes go astray,
And lost without no plan.

Technology rules and now are the tools,
To compose a little song.
Without a heart and worlds apart,
Is this so right or wrong?

The rose-tinted lens is not the cure,
To justify concern.
It's just that we have lost something,
Whenever will we learn?

DARKNESS

The darkness can be your friend,
No illumination to distract your thoughts.
A dark space, a moment, an episode,
It can bring you to full priority.
Then, see nothing more,
Only your images of convictions.

A MISSION

We are all on a mission,
To make this world seem right.
It is all in our decisions,
In need to stop the fights.

Of the ones who want to take it,
The beauty of our lands.
Then, claim It's theirs and just won't share,
They attack with new demands.

And proclaim a promise too,
That is when they are all through.
Your land is and they don't care,
Your land is now anew.

FREE WILL

It seems to be a perfect saying: "Free Will",
That mitigates all wrongs on Earth.
And used within an ordained breath,
Commenced or baptised from your birth.

"Free Will" to justify the loss,
No matter how, it can't be stopped.
For the sorrows and the human cost,
For warmth with sunshine, days are lost.

PLACE

I hale, you went to the right place,
A far different world.
Away from the inner-city grime.
Yes, these magical lands exist.
All though it will be many moons,
You will reach that place.
You will meet the ones who you anoint.

To bestow your beneficence among each other,
And then you will sure discover.
There are the ones who long to learn,
Your wealth of knowledge they still yearn.

The path is cleared from pain and tears,
You continue to fight without the fears.
You got there.
Well done!

ALIEN

An alien came down to Earth one day,
To see how we all lived.
The streets were full of cardboard homes,
A massive sigh he'd give.

The shops were empty, the folks were gone,
This left a poor impression.
He went back to his space craft buggy,
And flew in a new direction.

REFLECTION

TYPEWRITER

Type the words to create a theme,
Try to carve out that human dream.
Sentence, phrase with paragraph.
Tell a story to cry and laugh.

The typewriter is the one to say,
Your words of wisdom, novel or play.
Transfer your thoughts onto a page,
Release to fly, there is no cage.

The keys struck down with rampant speed,
The hunger fed to your machine.
Feeding words of woe and glory,
Your mind narrates to etch in story.

Typewriter alone without a plug,
Is still the one for writing the hook.
The tale, the event of a chosen idea,
Enlightens the soul from year to year.

FORGOTTON, SIMPLE.

Has 'simple' now been misplaced?
Is it now replaced with more functions?
We can send a rocket to space,
But now, we're at a strange new junction.

Simple flora grows in all directions,
But all eyes are aimed at the screen.
The aspiration with expectation,
Has become a brand-new dream.

Simple replaced with tablet and phone,
Yet, one day sadly, they'll be all alone.
Have they forgotten?

CARGO

The sea is grey and why not blue?
How did this all occur?
It's now become a dumping ground,
No one now seems to care.

A ship sails by into the night,
With troubled cargo stow.
All been gathered with neat intention,
To let this baggage go.

Into the watery pit of doom,
Too fool us all, you see.
That re-cycled goods can all end up,
Beneath our precious sea.

LET GO.

Have you ever had to let go?
Of that dear darling being.
Who you trusted, invested into your heart.
Yet, painful realisation of Paradise.
Just won't sustain,
But only in pain.
The bliss masks the greyness.
With animated Azura skies, high definition.
That temptation draws you, beckons you.
To another existence.
Utopian screen.

Beware, you are mightier and stronger.
You are adored, loved and needed by others.
In the real world.

BEAUTIFUL MINDS

Beautiful minds.
Blending the pallet with colours and shade.
Paint brush, stroking the blank paper.
That sheet first empty.
Becomes the object of purpose.
You now see the person.
Who relates to the function of creativity.
Who becomes our human friend.
Right the end, with purpose.

FIRE FIGHTER

Each day, I put fires out,
Then, to the rescue with a scream and shout.
To save a building,
To save a class.
The school is on fire,
How's it going?
You may ask.
Absolutely marvellous.

Not.

WHY?

Why is there so much confusion?
When all you want is a solution.
To troubled rooms now all around,
Emitting defiance with ugly sounds.
A new head comes in,
As 'Uncle Buck',
To turn it around,
Good Luck!

LOST CAUSE [Contract].

Do we abandon a lost cause?
Deemed not to translate into your expectation.
Do we just carry on?
Pretending witness out of sight.
Do we infer to,
Well, "it's not my problem".
Ignorance is bliss.
It is if you have misled your conscience.
Yet, you did see the deed underneath your watch.
This denial masks the real event.
But you do have a morality.
You do have an agreement with yourself.
With your soul, your inner being.
With your legacy.
This is a life contract.
Keep to it.

PROMISED LAND

They trek to find their promised land,
Through forest, mountain with desert sand.
With hungry need and thirsted tongue,
To seek their fortune, to be among them.

The seekers of a Promised Land,
Yet, the indigenous folk don't understand.
To how they survived to join the rest,
They wanted joy to share and invest.

The land on foot eventually ceased,
Now craft to float from somewhere East.
Their money spent to buy a space,
It will ensure a sailing to a place.

A risk to take a chance to make,
The Gods look down to give them grace.
The months go by to reach this hour,
They reach the waters to ivory towers.

A storm with rain gives them a miss,
They carry on with clouded bliss.
Then, find their shores to Promised Land,
They thank the Gods to kiss the sand.
Amen.

MOULDING MINDS

Is this the right place to be?
A building for moulding minds.
The moulding has set hard.
Like concrete blocks.
Fixed into a mindset of rebellious mode.
The switch has certainly jammed.
New reprogramming is needed here.
The folk facilitate an existence of denial.
With reframed patterns of reason.
A new rationale is here.
A new course to study and learn.
A new way to have your fingers burnt.
Yet please do not be spurned.
You are needed so!
Keep going.

DIGITAL EYE

The digital eye now rules,
With a simple click, it is easy and quick.
Your profile is just,
Smooth and slick.

Have we lost a generation,
Of folk who refuse to start?
With relationships and wooing tips,
The chip now replaces the heart.

LOSS

"When someone you love becomes a memory,
that memory becomes a treasure."

UNKNOWN

LEGACY

Your legacy is all you must give,
For when that last farewell comes.
You may leave behind a scripted -
Yet an animated spool of your existence.
Which runs for miles.
The DNA comes later -
Through your futures of genetic souls.
That legacy of memoir with human experience.
Becomes still, frozen to the second.
But still, the memories continue to share your legacy.
The spool, all to be replayed repeatedly.
Tears and laughter for sure.
A real best seller.
A real box office success.

We have all purchased that ticket.
We booked the seats.
We have the book.
Your legacy.

CIRCLE OF LIFE.

A circle of life,
we all play a part.
With happiness or strife,
Right from the start.

So, make it all count,
And seize your day.
And don't waste that gift,
Which comes your way.

SHOES

Cared and kept neatly silent and still,
Yet, it emits your energies, my sweet.
Shiny, polished, and gleaming with pride,
I still wait for you, to greet.

A constant daily reminder of your vibrant existence,
Now taken away.
You took that final flight to your new world,
That one-way ticket is no longer with me to stay.

Leather breaths, but lifeless, lonely and empty,
Can never be complete without your presence again.
I try a new one for measure, for size,
But they just will not fit, still evokes the pain.

That being could never fill your shoes,
They could never emulate you.
Will I ever move forward?
Will I ever start a new?

Those shoes could never be walked in ever more,
They could never be fitting for other than you.
I hang on to hope you will walk through that door,
Oh my God, I pray. What am I to do?

     LOSS

MILESTONES

We shared those glorious milestones,
Together, we conquered each quest.
We engaged with love and to atone,
To unite our love to invest.

Those seasons and moons they did fly,
Yet, we embraced those years with real love.
They're now taken within the blink of an eye,
I thank Heavens you were sent from above.

God made you that sweetest of being,
To awake with you every dawn.
To share the Blessings of kin folk,
To bring life to the world with newborn.

To share passions of animal desire,
To hold you in passionate embrace.
To stoke flames of lustful fire,
No other, could ever take your place.

But, darling those ghosts of your past,
They were lessons and not meant to last.
They can haunt with sorrowful grief,
But please take comfort and take belief.
That I so miss you.

WITHOUT YOU

I once was your flame,
But now it's never the same.
You guided me to a lonely place,
To open this door to an empty space.

I once was your sweetest desire,
But now you doused that passioned fire.
You show me to a lonely door,
But I still love you more and more.

Tis I, who now will hold that key,
That locks away the past.
The door slams tight with every night,
Will I ever last?

I once was your flame,
Yet now the world is tame.
Will I unlock my door again?
It will never be the same.

Without you.

LOVED AND LOST

It is better to have loved and lost,
Than to have never loved at all.
Its value is worth the cost,
No matter if love was small.

Love conquers all.

LOCKED AWAY

Like an old violin,
I feel locked away.
Never to be played,
To see the light of day.

The price of love I have paid,
Why do you not own my tune?
Has my music, seen better days?
I ask myself each moon.

Remember once it made our love,
The music you adored.
Together, like a golden glove,
Yet now denied applause.

Now you've locked me in a room,
You have learned a different song.
With a new melodic ballad and tune,
And I wonder for just how long.

You have found a new player now to woo,
To charm and flirt your smile.
A new book you make of melodies,
It will only be a while.

Before you learn a new song.

CALLING

When God calls you,
To be without pain.
His divine touch will heal you,
Your might will re-gain.

No more suffering,
No more prayers.
With God beside you,
With golden stairs.

EULOGY

From the cradle to the grave,
Your documentary proceeds on.
No hour a minute was wasted,
With daily moon and sun.

The years were crammed with goodness,
They followed you around.
An awe of majestic beauty,
Your presence would astound.

That dash between the date of birth,
To when you fell asleep.
Still packed with joys of who you are,
Those chronicles run deep.

You were the chosen one,
To share with us your mission.
To show us all, how to be,
To love without contrition.

You are dearly loved with esteem to you,
A beacon of virtue so bright.
Yet now dear God has chosen you,
To keep you in his sight.

Even the angels have welcomed you,
They adore you with your presence.
And know to just - how special you are,
Your righteousness, your essence.

Sweet Dreams.

GONE

To share our slumber with warmth once more,
Tis all I ever ask.
The aromas from your fragrant skin,
Etched in mind to ever last.

The hallowed beauty with breath so warm.
To reveal once more with thee,
To give an evening, morning kiss,
Each hour I always see.

Your physical form no longer there,
With empty coldness rest.
Your shadow has gone with the moon and sun,
Tis still a mighty test.

A day may come if I move on,
I know it's not this morn.
Oh, darling please, there is no ease,
For you my heart is torn.

Now you're gone with daily sun,
The Heavens now have a place.
For an angel from Earth, my mystic's worth,
My heart still leaves a space.
For you.

LOST

When losing someone,
It's like a piano without keys.
No more melody,
The piano rests in peace.

Gathering dust,
With closed lid.
No more tunes,
Now, all hid.

Locked away into my recall,
The stool sits empty,
The room is small,
Without you.

At night alone,
In my chair.
All to atone,
Is for you I care.

To hear you play,
Once again.
To hear you say,
"My lover, my mystical friend".

Just once again.

ARRIVAL WITH FAREWELL

You are waiting for that panged arrival,
Of your unique and blessed one.
Composure with profound reflection.
Filters through with muted awe.
Images past and present,
Animates your soul.
Dignified murmurs echo above your mindfulness.
The cathedral of condolence.
Music offers little solace.
But the heart remains in desolation.
There's healing of this hour.
Whispered muttering words of woe.
Fade to silent a freeze frame.
Your loved one is here.
To say a final farewell.
Accompanied with tearful eyes.
With hesitant breath.
Wetted cloth of silver droplets.
Lucidity strikes to the core.
The moment.
The real hour.
The real farewell.

NIGHT TIME

The darkness of bittered night,
Breeze again becomes chill.
Grass becomes grey and dull,
Frosted windowsill.

Blackened blanket of sky above,
Hides the stars behind.
Moon takes an evening break,
No light, you will not find.

My only lantern is of you,
You were my guiding star.
Another night to get through,
To wonder where you are.

The echoes of your words,
Filter through my head.
To lie alone with torment to own,
Within my barren bed.

LOST TODAY

Today, you lost your plan,
You can't change how things become.
You've lost ways to purge your darkness,
Your bleakness consumes you.

You have lost how to feed on life's nourishment,
You have lost how to drink nectar rain.
Yet, your loss is not an instalment,
You will find your happiness again.

OSCAR

Mobility static in time,
A snapshot of the final cut.
Yet you are to become that new leading role.
You have taken a new journey.
To a far distant picture land.
Away from this dull Earth.
You have distanced your existence.
No longer to star in daily life.
But to leap with joy in your new motion picture.
You are still the star.
Your debut appearance will win an Oscar.
In your new world.

DEPRIVED

The condition of being deprived,
Of someone special to you.
The condition of being denied,
Forever will be true.

When a loved one is just taken away,
Without reason, without goodbye.
To then feel a human treason,
Deflated with tearful cry.

No rationale could appease,
For me you held the key.
To happiness.

ADULT RIFF

They seemed to have lost each other,
Moved on to another life.
But they denied me of another,
To give me further strife.

They split into angered terms,
They never gave me a thought.
Now alone in this new home,
The sorrows this has brought.

I no longer see my folks,
They are so far away.
This adult riff with tainted split,
Oh please, just go away.

WHERE TO?

A loss of vision,
A loss of hope.
A wrong decision,
I cannot cope.

A loss of miles,
Just standing still.
A loss of smiles,
A loss of will.

Where to next,
I just don't know.
No phone to text,
Where will I go?

To be that one,
To be a king.
To be so happy,
To daily sing.

Where too?

COMPASSION

To lose the energy of prayer,
To lose the faith in you.
To lose the peace to wager war,
To lose a sea of blue.

To lose the love you keep,
To lose the gift of passion.
To lose the tears along with weep,
But please don't lose compassion.

DARKEST HOUR

In your darkest hours,
To grieve your loss.
Let spirits elope,
Let them cross.

Cross over to a place,
Where angels play.
Pray for their soul,
Each, every day.

The hour has chimed,
No more are they.
In your darkest hour,
It is OK.
To weep.

POCKET PICKING

It appears the new way to go,
To dig deep into their pocket.
Finding their ways to show,
To lose health for others to profit.

These losses manifest in grief,
We all must suffer the pain.
Then, a new loss with disbelief,
It will never be the same.

We have lost our faith in them,
Who wave their tainted wand.
They continue to seek mayhem,
To take from a national fund.

The loss has sought no reason,
To maintain a spiritual ease,
They continue to pick our pockets,
To continue to take as they please.

Pocket picking, picking a pocket,
It might sound just the same.
Do we lose our trust each day?
This is an unfair game.

Another loss.

HUMOUR

WITH SOME FOR YOUNGER READERS.

"To succeed in life, you need three things:
A wishbone, a backbone and a funny bone."

REBA McENTIRE.

A COUGH AND A SPLUTTER.

A cough and a splutter,
Is all I do.
The inhaler with lozenge,
Is my helpful crew.

The steroids do work,
With antibiotic shield.
I take every day,
Straight after a meal.

On my way -
To feel much better,
I listen to my body,
And follow the letter.

It must be working,
It must do the trick.
Because I'm getting the urge,
To dance with a kick.

HOLD ON.

Don't buy a turkey for Christmas,
Just open a tin of spam.
Hold on to your pennies this Christmas,
Then sing to 'Last Christmas' by Wham.

HAPPY NEW YEAR.

Just sending good wishes,
To have a great year.
Just sending you my love,
With laughter and tear.
To know you are wonderful.
To see your delight.
But I'm going to the opticians,
To check my eyesight.

FAIRY NIGHTS.

A fairy came to say, "hello",
One warm and summer's night.
And did a cartwheel on the lawn,
She was so slim and spright.

Her backflips were amazing,
My eyes could not believe.
The wonders of her sprightly charm,
I hoped she'd never leave.

Then she hovered in the sky,
To sprinkle stardust kisses.
Then she went and said, "goodbye",
But granted me magical wishes.

I wished for peace for everyone,
I wished for hunger's cure.
I wished that she would come back soon,
And cartwheel more and more.

HAVE YOU MET?

Have you ever met that one,
Who has grace and charm?
Of someone who believes they're wonderful,
 For you, there is alarm.

They think they are so perfect,
Retired and full of 'know.'
Yet, they expose a rudeness,
Your senses, they do grow.

So sad, to meet their vision,
As they just fill their pot.
For holiday funds and tea and buns,
And really, that's their lot.

KIRKALDY.

There was an old man from Kirkcaldy,
Who had the most stinkiest body.
He never did wash,
And ever talked posh.
And his undies were filthy and shoddy.

HUMOUR

REGINALD

A gent name Reginald Smythe,
Once went to the barbers in Clyth.
He had short back and sides,
With a smile open wide,
With a glee he just couldn't hide.

TONIC

A daily tonic of you,
Would lift me up so true.
Your daily hug,
And when we're snug,
With you I'm never blue.

GETTING DRUNK

Getting drunk in your underpants,
Is the best feeling ever.
But when you do it on the bus,
Now that's not very clever.

CILLA

One day, when I was in my house,
A knock came on the door.
Twas a six-foot gorilla,
Her name was Cilla,
And smiles she had galore.

She asked me nicely if I would play,
To skip outside the street.
I introduced her to my mates,
It really was a treat,

Everyone loved Cilla,
She charmed their parents too.
And very soon when it was June,
We met her sister Sue.

MAX

Max, the dog who liked to roam,
Always went walkies and always alone.
He trundled the streets,
He danced through the park.
And never came home,
Until it was dark.

ALL SORTS

It seems such a mixed-up jumble,
An array of variant sorts.
My thinking with logic so tragic,
With ideas of scrambling thoughts.

I'm confused oh what shall I do?
I really have not got a clue.
So, I take a deep breath,
With a spring in my step,
I'm still happy, and that's very true.

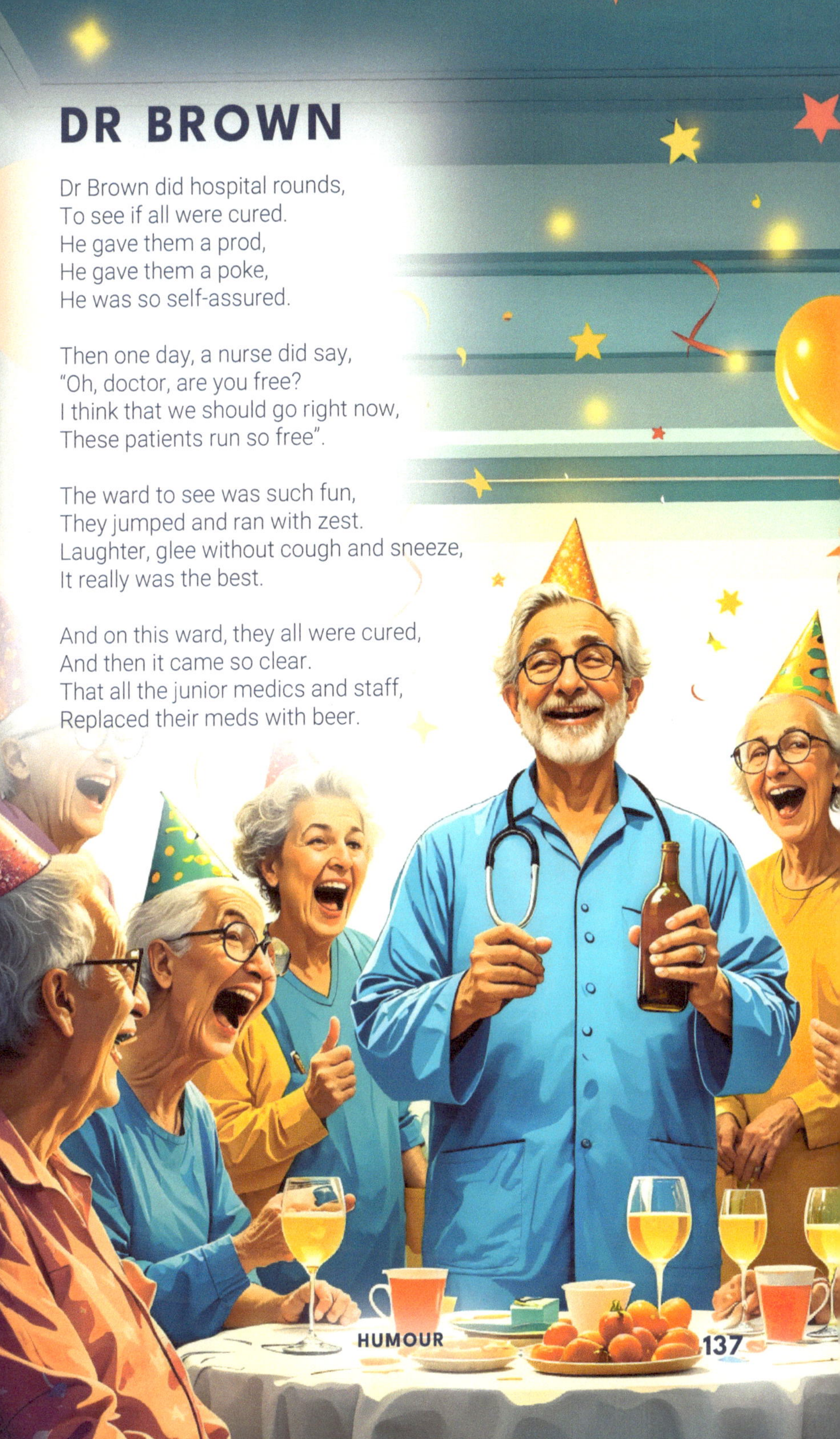

DR BROWN

Dr Brown did hospital rounds,
To see if all were cured.
He gave them a prod,
He gave them a poke,
He was so self-assured.

Then one day, a nurse did say,
"Oh, doctor, are you free?
I think that we should go right now,
These patients run so free".

The ward to see was such fun,
They jumped and ran with zest.
Laughter, glee without cough and sneeze,
It really was the best.

And on this ward, they all were cured,
And then it came so clear.
That all the junior medics and staff,
Replaced their meds with beer.

KNOCK ON DOOR

A knock on the door came one day,
And met with a snail who asked me to play.
I placed him away down the path,
Then I went to run a bath.

Six months later he's back at the door,
Then shouted at me,
"What was that for?"

Bum Bum.

MARCELL

The best-dressed camel you will see,
Always with glamour with chic was she.
She trots through the desert with elegant gait,
Always on time and never was late.

GINGERBREAD MAN

Gingerbread Fred,
Stayed in bed,
He did not want to rise.
He felt so glum and told his mum,
With saddened, tearful eyes.

"Why are they not wanting me?
Why have they changed my form?
I'm a Gingerbread man,
Of the biscuit clan,
They've certainly caused a storm".

RICKY THE RAT

Ricky the rat once saw a cat,
And ran to save his skin.
The cat chased by with evil eye,
To smile with menacing grin.

Ricky froze still and waited until,
To feel that he was safe.
When all was clear he lost his fear,
Then had some tea and cake.

DOSE

A daily dose of laughter,
Is really all you need.
To laugh with joy each girl and boy,
With chuckles more to feed.

Those belly laughs and hearty smiles,
That flows with seratone.
So please do, to join the queue,
And never again you'll moan.

SPANISH CLASS

The Spanish class it went so well,
They all did their revision.
To work upon their Spanish script,
They were certainly on a mission.

This lesson was a red flag,
To the Spanish bull.
They raced through all the questions,
It really was not dull.

Ole!

BRIDGET THE FIDGET

Bridget the fidget,
She could not keep still.
And darted around,
And raced up the hill.

Her legs were to the left,
Her legs were to the right,
She danced all around,
Twas a wonderful sight.

Her energy is prolific,
Her speed was so fast.
And Bridget the fidget,
All day, she would last.

WHOOOOOSH!!!

BUSTER BULL

Buster Bull was king of the farm,
He strutted around the field.
But he was kind and gentle,
He could sense the way you feel.

If you were sad and you felt down,
He'd come to say "hello",
After a chat with Buster,
You'd have a pleasant glow.

DONKEY DAVE

Donkey Dave enjoyed his hay,
Mixed with Weetabix.
Donkey Dave was not afraid,
Of his favourite mix.

With porridge oats and Marmite spread,
He loved to chomp his food.
Then washed it down with ginger pop,
All day, he loved to chew.

SIMPLE LIFE

A simple life is all I want,
No complicated folly.
I want to sing, laugh and dance,
Be happy and be jolly.

A roaring fire to warm my room,
A decent cup of tea.
With lively cheers without the tears,
That's all I want you to see.

To give mirth and glee to all I see,
Bring a smiles to their face.
To kiss my sweet, my darling treat,
Twould be my perfect place.

SNOWMAN

A snowman came to me one day,
To complain that he was cold.
His frosted eyes with no surprise,
Along with runny nose.

He asked me if he can come inside,
So, he could just warm up.
And so, I did without a bid,
But had to then clean up.

From a puddle of this snowman
All left was his hat and his scarf.
And so, I smiled to say goodbye,
Then I heard a laugh.

It was rather eerie.

ONE LINER

The 'one liner', designer for humour,
Now received with much weariness.
Nervous laughter is somewhat such gloomer,
To impede upon sheer merriness.

Social landscapes are reshaped and breaths lame,
The quelled staffroom is never the same.
We now see bellowed laughter disappear,
Have we created a platform for fear?

But I will still tell my joke,
To all my family and all my folk.
To make them all laugh,
With colleagues and staff,
Until I keel over and croak.

UNWELL

Oh mum, oh dad,
I don't feel well,
I am feeling rather queezy.
My throat is sore, my tummy aches,
I tell you, this aint easy.

I just cannot go to school,
And do my work in class.
But can I please stay in bed,
This is all I ask.

But then I smell that toast,
With marmaladed bread.
And so, I feel much better,
I'll go to school instead.

CHARM

I am the one who has this charm,
It gets me through the hours.
I buy my love sweets and candy,
I even buy her flowers.

But once I was so naughty,
I made my lover mad.
And so, I gave her chocolates,
She said, "you're not that bad".

PET GORILLA

MY poor gorilla did not feel well,
He coughed and sneezed all day.
The vet came out to check him out,
To ensure he was OK.

With medicine, massage and gentle care,
The gorilla regained his might.
And the very next day, he went out to play,
With his palls to fly his kite.

NAPPY DAYS

The nappy was placed upon the floor,
Should I pick it up?
My baby sister took it off,
The pong it would not stop.

I shouted to my mum,
Before the pong does spread.
I think I'll pinch my nose so tight,
And leave the room instead.

POLLY PARROT

Polly Parrot swore one day,
He was a naughty boy.
The air was blue, I swear it's true,
My mum he did annoy.

We took him to the local vet,
And told them of this tale.
They laughed so hard with high regard,
They certainly all did wail.

But soon, they solved the problem,
And soon, they all did make.
A fixture for its potty mouth,
Then, it wrapped its beak with tape.

DR JONES

Dr Jones had funny bones,
He made his patients giggle.
When he took their temperature,
He liked to dance and wiggle.

He would rest the patient on the bed,
To check their heartbeat too.
Then would joke with all the folk,
His patients formed a queue.

To have their daily dose of fun,
To laugh and chuckle each day.
Dr Jones he never moans,
He always skipped and played.
Next Please!

MORE TO PONDERS

If you are interested in reading more of Steve's work, please contact him via email, Facebook, or at the Life Ponders Poetry website,

lifeponderspoetry.com.
info@lifeponderspoetry.com.

MORE TO
PONDERS

Book 4 will be out soon.

LIFE
PONDERS
POETRY

If you have enjoyed Steve's poetry and wish to know more, please contact him via email, Facebook, or the Life Ponders Poetry website.

Lifeponderspoetry.com

Info @lifeponderspoetry.com

Printed in Great Britain
By London Book Publisher

LIFE PONDER POETRY

I continue to write with mystical scribe,

With more life to ponder to seek through an eye.

To share a new vision to how we get through,

The trials of existence, we encounter so true.

"I see your true colours shing through".
Such lovely meaningful words speaking
to the soul which I can pick up & read over &
over again. I love the honesty & no holding
back! The artwork is fantastic too!
KATH STRATHDEE

"A poetry book that touches every emotion,
And left me wanting more".
Steve's gifted soul shines throughout his
book of life poems. Emotive, thought
provoking, who can't have been moved by
the passion that oozed from the section of
Love, Lust & desire, I realised I hadn't
taken a breath for about three pages.
SHERRY SLATER

"Beautiful poetry which is inciteful and
spiritual".Steve looks at the beauty of what we
may miss out on. Beautiful illustrations to
draw attention to the facts from his work.
Very talented and blessed.
NICOLA SUMMER

"There isn't anything that cannot
be recommended in this book".
Everything is just a hundred percent true to life.
I absolutely love these. They are so real to life.
LORRAINE TOOVEY

"Excellent pages of poetry".
I love reading Steve's poems. Such lovely lyrics. It takes
a lovely mind to write like this.
LORRAINE DAVIS

"Wonderful poetry that reflects upon
 the rich tapestry of life."
with all its joys, sorrows and challenges, and the world
in which we inhabit. The author conveys heartfelt
sentiments of love, loss, inspiration with reflection. Not
forgetting humour, enabling the
reader to understand that every choice, experience and
relationship matters and enriches our lives.
I highly recommend!
MONICA